ABOUT THE AUTHORS

Gabrielle Gloury's career in social policy and secondary teaching has honed her astute observations, research and professional writing skills. A feminist, political junkie and self-confessed sports tragic, *Girls Change the Game* is her first venture into the world of adolescent fiction. After a decade of secondary teaching, Gabrielle held senior positions at Victoria University, Victorian public sector and the Aboriginal and Torres Strait Islander Commission.

Michael Hyde mainly writes for adolescents and YA. He gained a PhD with his memoir of the sixties, *All along the Watchtower*. Prior to his 20 years lecturing in Professional Writing and Children's Literature at Victoria University, he spent 25 years as a secondary school English teacher. Although a full-time writer, Michael continues to present writing workshops for students and teachers across Australia.

Also by Michael Hyde

Footy Dreaming

All Along the Watchtower (Memoir)

Change the Game Series

Winning Streak

Finals Chance

Arch Rivals

Mud and Rain

Rough Play

Champions Cup

Surfing Goliath

Hey Joe

Tyger Tyger

MAX

Eagle

Morrison and Mr Moore

For all the girls and women who loved the game but never had a chance to play it

— GG & MH

First published by Ford Street Publishing,
162 Hoddle Street, Abbotsford, Melbourne Victoria Australia

2 4 6 8 10 9 7 5 3 1

Ford Street website: www.fordstreetpublishing.com
First published 2023

National Library of Australia Cataloguing-in-Publication entry:
Authors: Gloury, Gabrielle; Hyde, Michael
Title: Girls Change the Game / First Game Back Gabrielle Gloury & Michael Hyde

ISBN: 9781922696304 (paperback)

A catalogue record for this book is available from the National Library of Australia

Cover and text design: © Joanne Marchese
Printed in China by Tingleman Pty Ltd

Aussie Rules

by

GABRIELLE GLOURY   MICHAEL HYDE

FORD ST

Westpark Scorpions

Westpark Scorpions Under 14 Girls' Football Team

Motto: ***A Champion Team can always beat a Team of Champions***

Coach: Rita

Runner: Andy

Manager/Medico: Anna

Doctor: Vanessa

Player Positions:

Back	Hannah	Laini	Beth
Half-Backs	Holly	Chandra	Matilda
Centre	Sophie		
Half-Forwards	Ava	Grace	Ruby
Forwards	Zoe	Talia	Thao
Followers	Heidi	Emma	Elly
Interchange	Poppy, Maya, Ivy, Alexandra		

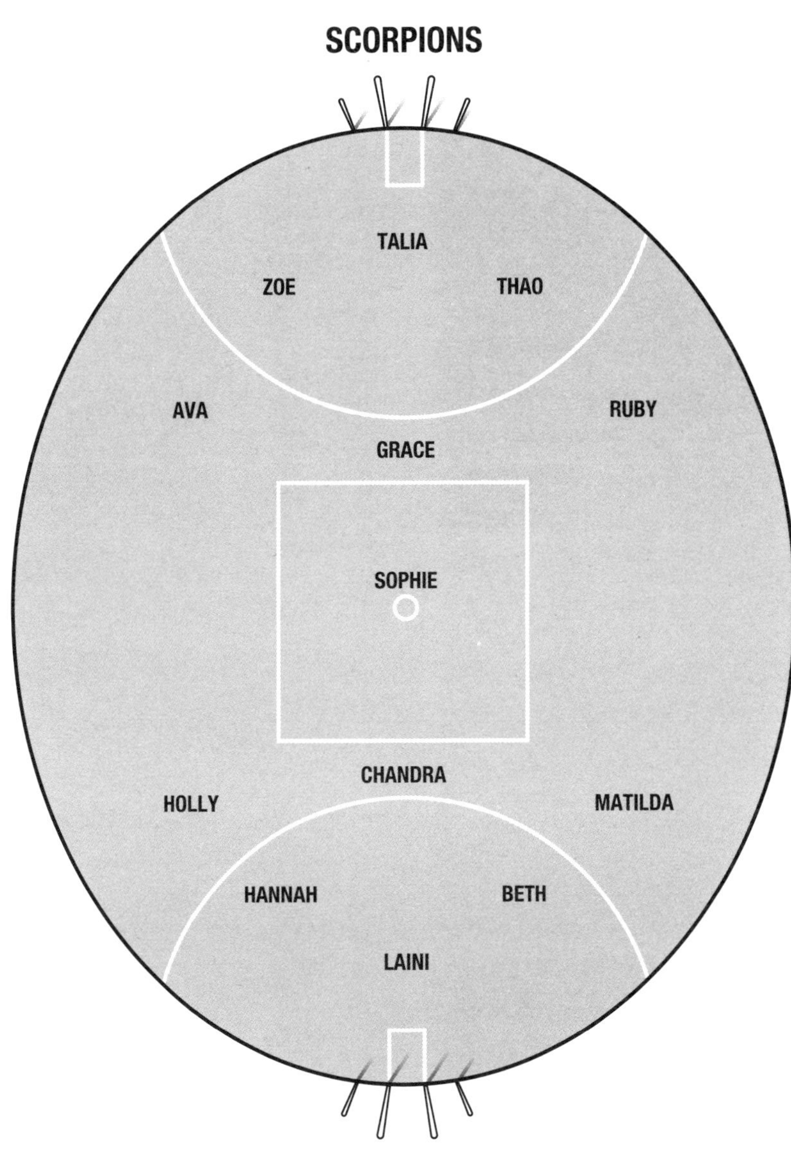
SCORPIONS
TALIA
ZOE
THAO
AVA
RUBY
GRACE
SOPHIE
CHANDRA
HOLLY
MATILDA
HANNAH
BETH
LAINI
RIVERSIDE DEVILS

BEFORE THE GAME IN THE CHANGE ROOMS

Well, who could believe it? The Westpark Under 14 Scorpions Girls are back. The Under 14 girls' football team to be precise. There's been so many obstacles and difficulties over the last year, Covid being the main thing responsible for games being cancelled or called off in the previous season, and finally the season having to be abandoned after a number of lockdowns. Not the same thing as playing the game – but now the girls are back!

And you can feel the joy in the change rooms. Sure, there's a bit of unease and some unfamiliarity. Who could blame these girls and their friends and families after what they and the whole community have gone through? A number of the players and their parents have actually gone through Covid, some worse than others. A few have had long Covid as well. Many are still getting over it.

The club has kept contact with everybody, mainly through Facebook, while some of the girls have stayed in touch through Instagram and TikTok. Not the same thing as actually playing the game, but at least it helped with the isolation. A number of the girls have suffered the hardship of contracting Covid and experienced lockdown and isolation, so it was a really hard year. To be frank, wild horses couldn't keep these girls – these amazing Westpark Scorpions Girls – from getting into training and turning up today to get into the action again.

The rooms are alive with chatter and gossip, laughing about new hairstyles and particularly Ruby, who has her head buzzed into a crewcut. The girls are all rubbing their hands on her head and teasing her. But Ruby is way too cool to be worried by that and just laughs it off, saying that the others must be jealous. Thao reckons she's going to get hers done in the same way. Thao's parents might have something to say about that!

'Looks so tough.' She laughs. 'Opposition will think twice before they take us on.'

Grace agrees. 'Might scare a few of the freaked-out players but I don't think it'll worry Belle.' She's referring to one of the strongest girls in the Riverside Devils team they're up against today.

Belle is known for her ferocious attack on the ball, strength and tackling. She is their gun forward, kicking goals from everywhere. But she plays fair and is a cousin of Sophie's, the Scorpions' centre. Fair or not, Belle is known for putting the fear of God into any team she plays against. The new girl, Laini, will be her opponent today so she's not laughing too much.

Sadly, there's been a few big changes. Bec and Jasmine have moved to the Under 16s, which means the Scorps have lost a lot of football experience.

Isabella and her mother moved away to the country during the pandemic, where Isabella's mum found work. Very sadly, her grandmother, Lizzie, has since died. Lizzie had been at most of the practice games and was there at that fantastic game where the Scorpions beat the unbeaten Ravens Under 14 Girls. One of their first games in the competition.

The place in the change room where she sat in her wheelchair seems lost and lonely, and no one mentions it but Lizzie's presence can still be felt.

However, a new breath of fresh air has come along. Laini, Maya and Alexandra (Alex for short) have joined the team. Laini only got into footy in the last year but has brought much talent to the side. She's short but takes no backchat and has delivered some grunt. Maya is a First Nations girl with amazing athletic ability and can run all day, while Alexandra crossed over from the Ravens because she thought she might get more of a run with the Scorpions. The old coach, Brenda, has had to take time off to look after her unwell mother but found a new coach, Rita, who is a bit younger and who also played a few seasons with the Darebin Falcons. Brenda's daughter, Ivy, is still in the team and Brenda will get along to watch the Scorpions when she can.

Rita brought a number of new ideas and over the last six months introduced herself to the team online. She's done weekly check-ins via Zoom to monitor the girls' fitness, which really helped during isolation. She also suggested a few running exercises the girls could do when they were allowed out of their homes, plus some exercises they could do while at home. Rita also used several training drills via Zoom to help the girls' kicking style and handball. She's clearly had many chats with the old coach, Brenda, who advised Rita as to who the new leadership group should be. That group consisted of Zoe, Beth and Heidi, and online they have had many discussions with Rita concerning the approaching season.

The new leadership group are more than good friends. They seem to have taken on their role with relish and hope to introduce better on-ground leadership – something that the new coach has emphasised. We'll see if it makes a difference today.

And so the new-ish Scorpions Under 14 Girls' team has slowly taken shape. Their past glories and new team structures will certainly be tested today. Scorpions have lost some of their most experienced players and both teams seem to have different styles of play. A lack of practice matches might affect the teams, but we will see.

While the Devils like to control territory, the Scorpions play more of a chaos game, pushing and surging the ball forward to their 50 and then focussing on short sharp deliveries into their forward line. It's going to be interesting to see how both teams succeed with their game plan. The Scorpions have a lot of run in their team and have been made faster with the new inclusions of Laini and Alex.

It's one thing to thrive on a chaos game, but it takes a great deal of concentration and daring play to pull it off. We'll see how much the Scorpions Girls have improved and gained some footy maturity since the past season. Not to mention all the interruptions they and other teams have had to cope with.

Getting close to kick-off time. The twins, Ava and Poppy, hurriedly finish off braiding each other's hair. Old habits and old superstitions don't die. Chandra once again is taping her ankles. Her younger years playing soccer certainly took their toll on them but so far she's stayed with her new love, footy.

The parents are there but as the new coach starts to call the girls together, the mums, dads, helpers, stepdads and supporters move out of the way to the back of the room. Rita has asked Zoe, the captain, to collect the girls' phones into Rita's backpack. Insta, Snapchat, texting and TikTok are still not allowed in the change rooms until after the game. Zoe's little brother, Dylan, trots after his big sister who he clearly hero-worships. No doubt, after playing little kids' Saturday morning footy, we'll see him out there playing for the Scorpions in the future.

Andy, the runner, is here again organising his stuff. So too is his daughter, Heidi, who has played such an important role in this club, especially this year in the leadership group.

Anna, the manager and medico, is still here keeping the team organisation running smoothly. But there's a new helper this time around – Vanessa, a doctor friend of Rita's, the new coach. Vanessa never played footy in her day but loved it, so she took on umpiring as a way to help her pay her uni fees. She's been brought on board to keep an eye on the girls but she's mainly there to help with any head knocks. Good to see they're taking this stuff seriously. We'll stop talking for a minute to listen to the coach who's about to address the girls.

'Well, girls. There have been times when we never thought we could have a normal life again. And by normal I especially mean playing footy. Some of you are nervous playing again. For one or two of you, it's your first game with the Scorpions. Don't worry about that, because it's my first game as your new coach. Brenda did a fantastic job in your first year and you pulled off some amazing victories.

'I've been in touch with all of you over the last months, especially with the leadership group of Zoe, Beth and Heidi. The Devils are a very experienced team and clear favourites for this year. That means there's more pressure on them than there is on us. They know we're not afraid of tough competition, and they don't quite know what to expect. We've practised and practised our new style and now's the time to see how it works.

'Enough talk from me. Thanks for taking me on as your coach. We – all of us – the President, Stephanie Pellegrino, supporters, helpers, families, are right behind you. Let's do them proud! Let's go!'

The roar from inside the rooms can be heard outside on the ground where the Devils lie waiting.

FIRST QUARTER

Siren sounds and off we go into the new season. Let's see if the Scorpions can go even further than they did the last time they played – see how much effect Covid has had on both teams.

Ball goes up and an unbelievable leap from Heidi in the ruck. Like she's on springs! Doesn't bother with tap, just belts the ball forward where it's picked up by Thao who handballs directly to Grace who runs into an empty goal and slams it through. What a start to the Scorpions' new season. Twenty seconds for the first goal! You can hear the roar of the crowd.

	GOALS	BEHINDS	TOTAL
Westpark Scorpions	1	0	6
Riverside Devils	0	0	0

Now that's what we call a great start. Wow! That'll set the cat amongst the pigeons.

Ball back in the centre. Umpire bounces but it careers offline and out of the centre circle. Looks like the umpy is a bit rusty. Never mind. She throws it up and the rucks go at it. Tap by the Devils' ruck, Maggie, who wins it and ball bounces free. The play is out on the wing. Ball in contention. Ava gathers, dodges, weaves, turns, lovely handball to Talia who hurriedly gets boot to ball. Comes to Scorpions half-forward Grace who has no time to get rid of the ball and is descended on by Devils onballers. Ump takes the ball. Up it goes again and Ava snares the ball out of the pack but it goes off the side of her boot and lands in the hands of the Devils' half-back who handballs nicely to a running teammate, who evades a lunging tackle by Elly and drives it deep into her forward 50. Out comes Laini, the new girl in the Scorps' team, who takes a diving mark. No guts, no glory for this girl. How courageous is that? Must've slid five metres. She gets up. Does a clever little kick sideways. Dangerous but it's carried out perfectly. She had a reputation before she moved to the Scorpions for toughness and a take-no-prisoners attitude.

Meanwhile, Matilda has got the ball in her hands. Lots of hesitation. Look out! She didn't see the Devils' forward pocket and she's gone. Holding the ball. Free kick to Devils. She goes back, only 20 metres out, looks confident. Launches and through the middle! Devils' answering goal.

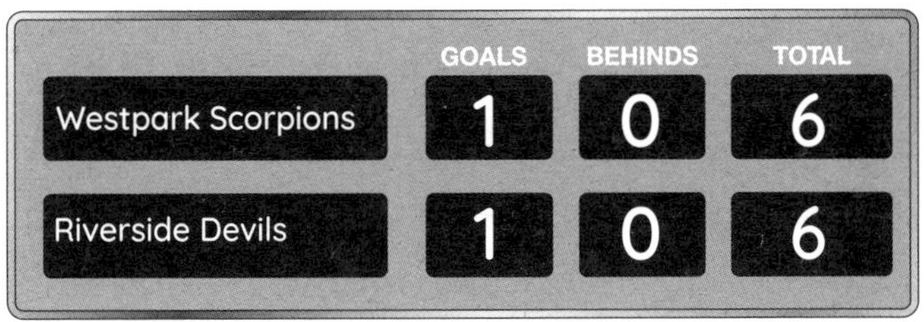

Two goals in the first 90 seconds of the game. We're in for a good one today.

Scorpions look a bit dejected but the leadership team – Zoe, Beth and Heidi – get around the girls and tell them, 'Heads up, work hard, it's early days.'

Okay. Game starts again. Another beautiful tap by Devils' ruck, Maggie, but ball stolen by Sophie who does a neat handpass to Maya who has just come onto the ground, replacing Elly. Coach has made an early change here, recognising they need more speed around the ball. And Maya certainly delivers. She's tackled, slips out of it and she's away. We were told this First Nations girl had speed but look at her go! She puts on the afterburners, bounces the ball once, twice and over to Thao who's been out on her own for what seems like ages. Thao stops. Nothing on offer up forward, so she kicks sideways to Zoe who gets into trouble. A lot of trouble. It's now three-on-one here in the Scorpions' forward area. Zoe wants to get it to Talia in the 10-metre square but there's no lead so she simply bangs it forward, heads towards the boundary and it rolls over. The Devils' crowd is screaming for an intentional out-of-bounds. Umpire runs towards the boundary umpire. No indication as yet whether it will be a throw-in or a free to the Devils for intentional out-of-bounds.

Will the umpire call it as intentional out of bounds and give a free to the Devils?

Go to page 16

OR

Will the umpire see it as not intentional out of bounds and call for the ball to be thrown in?

Go to page 24

You decided that it was an intentional out-of-bounds by the Scorpions and a free is awarded to the Devils.

Devils' back Isla takes the free kick and quickly sends it back towards the centre. A short pass into the Devils' forward area sees a strong mark by Devils' onballer, Jo. Looks like she is taking a very long shot for goal. It will be a prodigious kick to pull off. Forty-five metres? I don't think she's got it in her. Looks terribly confident. Yes, she's going for it. Big drop punt that looks good off the boot but lands well short. Well, she can't be blamed for having a go. Ball lands in a big pack, all hands and legs, and somehow, Belle gets boot to ball in there and it goes through . . . for a behind.

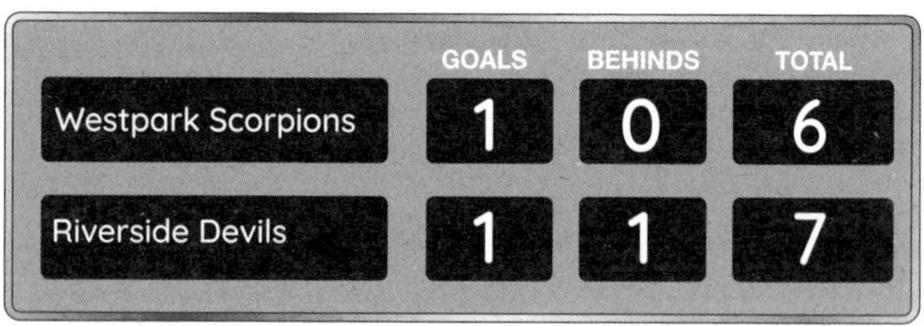

	GOALS	BEHINDS	TOTAL
Westpark Scorpions	1	0	6
Riverside Devils	1	1	7

Kickout by Hannah. Short kick. Umpire calls 'Play on'. Not the required fifteen metres. What a mistake! Hannah drops her head in embarrassment at her kick. Shocking slip-up for a back. Beth doubles back and goes once more to Hannah. Now she takes off and drives it to the wing where a big pack has formed. Devils mark Hannah's kick but the siren has sounded for the end of the quarter.

Girls head towards the boundary. Andy hurries up some of the stragglers. Coach Rita is impatiently waiting for the girls to get drinks and come together. Dylan is busying himself with handing out drinks. He's clearly loved by the girls.

Rita tells them that so far so good but they're not working hard enough moving the ball forward. That's the brand they've practised and now they have to execute it. Scorpions' quick movement of the ball forward will give their forward line plenty of opportunities. Too slow and the Devils will be able to organise themselves in defence. Rita takes Hannah aside and tells her not to focus on the kick-in mistake. It's easy for players to get stuck in negative thinking.

Beth and Zoe drag the girls into a tight bunch. 'Hands in. Go Scorpions!!!'

It's only the early stages of the game but these two teams seem incredibly well-matched. Devils have a better working forward line while the Scorpions have got their running game working well with lots of linkups by hand and foot. There's a lot of speed in the Scorpions' team.

SECOND QUARTER

Siren sounds to start the second quarter. The ball is bounced and the Scorpions win it out of the centre. Sophie is in and under. Cleared to Ruby who passes it wider to Ava who, with great awareness, sees Zoe calling for the ball. Another beautiful field kick. Hits the chest of Talia and now handballs to Sophie, the Scorpions' speedster, who has kept running from the centre bounce. She collects without missing a beat, dodges a Devils' big defender, gets to 30 and slots it! Scorpions' goal. What a display of hard running by Sophie. What incredible movement of the ball.

	GOALS	BEHINDS	TOTAL
Westpark Scorpions	2	0	12
Riverside Devils	1	1	7

Wowser. Moved it fast and precise. Looks like the Scorpion Girls have taken their coach's advice at quarter time to heart.

There's a runner out to the Devils' onballers. I can imagine what she's telling them. I suspect they took the Scorpions too lightly. Their key ruck Maggie is nodding furiously and moves in for the ball-up. It's thrown up, rucks work hard with no clear winner. Whistle blows. Free kick in the centre to Zoe for being held. Zoe takes no time and kicks to Elly who has just come back on, replacing Maya. She misses the mark. Players descend on her, messy pack forms and the ump calls for a ball-up. Comes down to Talia and now another free is called. Not sure what that was for. Scorpions' Heidi takes the free. Hesitates and then goes for a long bomb towards goal. Almost a mark there. Out to the pocket and Ruby pursues it to the boundary, working in a phone box here. Manages to keep it in. She picks up the ball, surrounded by Devils' defenders, and over to Grace with a quick kick who slams it through. Goal! Another goal for the Scorpions. This is getting ridiculous.

	GOALS	BEHINDS	TOTAL
Westpark Scorpions	3	0	18
Riverside Devils	1	1	7

Such an inexperienced team and they're handing a lesson to the experienced, older team, the Devils.

Devils' coach is yelling instructions from the bench. The Scorpion Girls are giving high fives but Heidi and Zoe are telling them it's no time to celebrate. Head down, tail up, work hard is the advice.

Again, we're back in the centre.

Ball-up. First tackle. Another ball-up. Devils desperate for possession game. Moving it quickly now. The Devils have clearly been told not to worry about kicking it down the line. Devils onballer boots it straight into the 50-zone but marked by Scorpions' defence, Chandra. It's often what happens with wild kicks. Kick and hope for the best but no hope there. The Scorpions are away again but a tackle sees the ball in space. Devils' player Jo gathers, shimmies and gets away, delivering to their forwards. Unfortunately, it was a scrubby kick but Devils are keeping it in their zone. Devils' full-forward Belle collects it but too far out. She has time to think about direction. She kicks into the pocket. There's two-on-one. Confusion reigns. Finally the Scorpions' back – Hannah – does a short handball to Laini who runs to the flank. With nowhere to go she decides to go backwards. Pokes at the ball. Dangerous move. Devils intercept and now they dribble the ball towards the goal. Looks like it's going to go through. Defence is working overtime. Scorpions' defender Beth stops it short, only a metre from the goal line. Now Belle crashes through and somehow gets a toe poke to the ball with Scorpions' defence frantic. Going to be touch-and-go here. The ball rolls through but Scorpions are saying it was touched.

Does the umpire rule it as touched and call it a behind?

Go to page 40

OR

Does the umpire rule it as a goal?

Go to page 47

You decided that it was not intentional out of bounds and the ball is thrown in.

Looks like it's a throw-in. Boy, the Devils' fans are not happy and are booing big time. Not really a great look for junior football. It simmers down. Good that we get hardly any ugly behaviour at these games. Devils' fans still upset. Especially because it's close to the Scorpions' goal. Ball thrown in, up goes Heidi. Strong girl. Has soft hands and gets a tap straight to Elly who roves beautifully, facing away from goal and at a 60-degree angle, almost impossible, snaps over her shoulder and sneaks through another goal to the Scorpions.

	GOALS	BEHINDS	TOTAL
Westpark Scorpions	2	0	12
Riverside Devils	1	0	6

Game starts in the middle again.

Emma copped a big hip and shoulder and she's not getting up. Tries but is a bit wobbly. Waving to the trainer. No concussion here but she's not in a good way. Yep, she's going off. Looks kind of okay but is now in the hands of the doctor, Vanessa, and Anna. They're not sure whether there was a head clash. Looks like Scorpions brought on a doctor to their team with good reason. Head knocks are a priority at any level. Lots has changed over the last years, thank heavens – all junior players wear helmets these days. Poppy replaces Emma.

Back to the game. Ivy, who has replaced Thao, is in possession but run down by Devils' onballer before she can get it forward. Swirling tackle, forcing Ivy to drop the ball. Free kick to Devils. Can go for goal. Big kick needed here. Probably beyond her abilities. Takes the kick but ball swerves out to her right going for distance. Unfortunately, it slides across the face of goal. Behind.

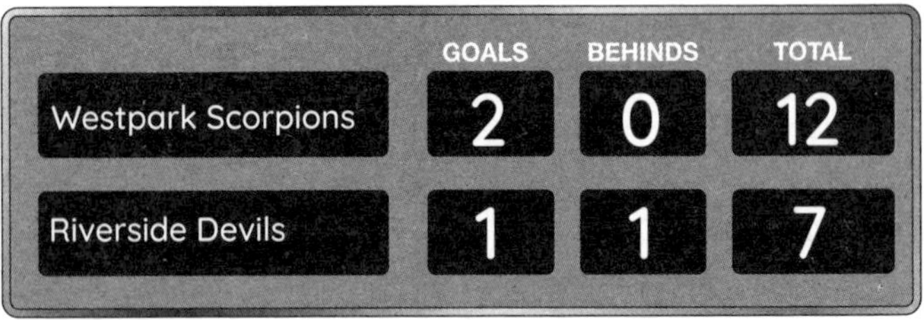

	GOALS	BEHINDS	TOTAL
Westpark Scorpions	2	0	12
Riverside Devils	1	1	7

Scorpions' back, Matilda, wastes no time and kicks out. Shocking kick. Another mistake by the Scorpions' backs. Ball comes to no one but players from both sides quickly respond and descend on the ball. Devils are in and under. Small Devils' forward gets it. Snaps out of the pack. Goal to the Devils and they take the lead by one point. Devils' players high-five each other as they celebrate that goal.

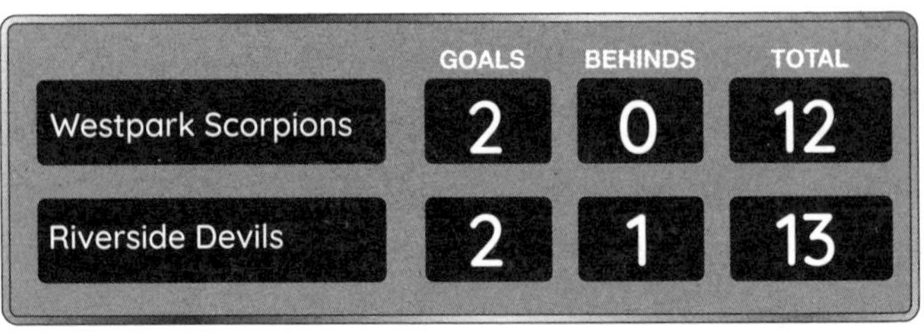

	GOALS	BEHINDS	TOTAL
Westpark Scorpions	2	0	12
Riverside Devils	2	1	13

Scorpions' Matilda who took the kick-out looks really upset with herself.

Her dad, Joe, a regular part of the Scorpions' crowd, yells to his daughter to concentrate on the game and not on her mistakes. Matilda waves her dad away. She's disappointed with herself but more embarrassed by her father. Not unusual for kids to be embarrassed by their parents. Joe is known for his noisy barracking and along with Chandra's dad, excellent BBQ food.

Siren sounds end of first quarter.

Quarter time and Scorpions gather around. Coach Rita has asked supporters to not come onto the ground. Says it distracts the girls and some of the parents and carers can't help themselves in handing out advice. Most of the supporters have taken this on board quite happily. A few have been disgruntled. Rita gathers her girls in close and congratulates them on their first quarter. Rita and the rest of Matilda's teammates aren't too worried by Matilda's mistake. They know on any day, any of them can make plenty of errors.

Rita's advice this time is for the girls to maintain their concentration. Good advice because even in the women's leagues you can see teams start to lose their advantage and momentum when their concentration begins to wane.

'All hands in,' says Rita. 'Scorpions!!!'

SECOND QUARTER

Siren goes for start of the second quarter. Ball-up.

Fight for the ball in the centre which continues out to the wing. Holly and Sophie are two-on-one here and then Sophie yanks the ball out of the hands of Devils' mid, thinks she's away but is run down and now Scorpions have got themselves into trouble. Maybe a chance for the Devils. Their ruck Maggie might go long here. Beautiful leap by Devils' forward on shoulders and brings it down with a thump. Handballs to a teammate running past while on the ground but she's not in the clear and there's one tackle after another. Out to the boundary line and now the race is on. Holly collects the ball. Short kick but pass intercepted by Devils' half-forward who might go back and have a shot. Has she got enough penetration with the kick? Not enough. Comes to ground. Ball not sitting. Scorpions' back, Beth, kicks it out of mid-air. Allows Devils' onballer to come in. She could be on here. She decides to tap it to her Devils' teammate who kicks deep into the 50 but wonderful mark by Laini in defence. Gee, she's been good. Gets it out of defensive zone again. It's anybody's ball. Scorps are under pressure. But now Devils come yet again with a wobbler almost to the goal but great mark again by Hannah. Whistle blows. It might be a mark but Devils' forwards are yelling that their full-forward Belle was shepherded out of the play.

Was the Devils' player Belle shepherded out of play? Free kick to the Devils.

Go to page 32

OR

Was the Devils' player Belle not shepherded out of play? Hannah's mark stands.

Go to page 55

You decided Devils' player Belle was shepherded out of play. Free kick to the Devils.

Tough decision by the umpire. Could've gone either way. But the umpires usually get it right and from where we saw it, Belle was definitely shepherded out.

So it's a quick no-nonsense goal with Belle sending the ball over the spectators' heads and into the carpark.

Goal to the Devils. Now the Scorpions will have to get that spark back to regain the lead.

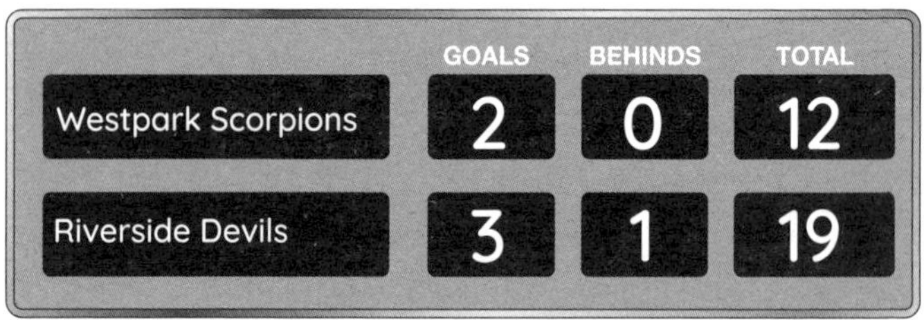

	GOALS	BEHINDS	TOTAL
Westpark Scorpions	2	0	12
Riverside Devils	3	1	19

Yes, another goal to the Devils. Scorpions have been outstanding, considering the strength and experience of the Devils, but they will need to stay in touch with the Devils and not let them get too far ahead on the scoreboard.

Ball back to the centre. Bounce. Rucks go at it. Ball being fought for. Sophie grabs the arm of Devils' centre. That's holding and Devils get the free. They're going to have to mix things up here. They don't want to become predictable at this stage. Margin is at seven points. Decides to head out to the wing but a scramble sees another ball-up. Heidi taps it down to Elly. Strong tackle on her and she goes down. She's not getting up. In a bit of pain with her shoulder which took the full weight of the fall. Let's hope it's not a dislocation or something more serious. Game continues. Devils lay another tackle. They're playing a close-checking game. Devils lay another tackle. Scorpions need the game to open up to have any chance. In fact, the only chance at the moment. Ball bounces into Devils' forward pocket. Devils' forward snaps but it's only a behind.

	GOALS	BEHINDS	TOTAL
Westpark Scorpions	2	0	12
Riverside Devils	3	2	20

Scorpions go better when the game opens up and they can get some movement into the action. Quick kick-out by Beth and Chandra marks. Plenty of space and she almost ambles her way along towards the wing, then a long kick into the half-forward area where a contested mark is taken by Poppy. Look out! Devils' onballer does not like the ump's decision and has a bit to say to the umpire. Umpire dissent and Poppy gets a 50-metre penalty. The Devils' supporters do not like that! Poppy takes her shot at goal. Bending away. No, it's through. Poppy's first goal and don't

	GOALS	BEHINDS	TOTAL
Westpark Scorpions	3	0	18
Riverside Devils	3	2	20

the rest of her team love it. She's mobbed down there.

A two-point game. Not too far away from half-time. That last shot would've stopped the Devils' run that seems to have increased since quarter time.

Back in the centre and Sophie takes no time in ripping the ball out of a strangle of hands. It's out to Ruby and she takes off with a slick overlap being provided by two other teammates. They take it straight through the middle and a bullet-like kick allows Thao to take the ball on her chest. Beautiful pass laces out. That's what forwards love. Thao walks back. Takes a quick look at the goalposts and sends it on its way. It's a miss. Nearly went out of bounds on the full. But a behind, nevertheless.

	GOALS	BEHINDS	TOTAL
Westpark Scorpions	3	1	19
Riverside Devils	3	2	20

Runner Andy has told the players it's only a minute to go till half-time. Devils' back Isla gets it going again. Long kick down the corridor but a screaming mark by Scorpions' Holly who climbed on backs and took the ball out of thin air. Crowd whistles and roars in approval. Holly looks for what's on offer. Thumps it out to Matilda, who sidesteps her opponent and goes for a run. One bounce, two bounces and passes to Grace. No one on the mark so she gains another ten metres and goes for goal and misses everything. Out of bounds on the full. These misses might come back to haunt the Scorpions.

That siren for half-time's going to go any second. Devils want to get it up their end. Devils' back Isla takes the kick. Comes off the side of her boot! Straight into the hands of Scorps captain, Zoe. Nobody there to stop her. Turns around and pops it through. Scorpions back in front. Now that's really going to hurt the Devils. And there's the half-time siren.

Probably good timing for the Devils who can't seem to take a trick at the moment.

	GOALS	BEHINDS	TOTAL
Westpark Scorpions	4	1	25
Riverside Devils	3	2	20

HALF-TIME

Amidst the bustle of the rooms, Rita has a quick word to the leadership group of Beth, Zoe and Heidi. Even with that last goal, the Scorpions are wasting opportunities which are hard to come by. Rita feels like they need more open play and more run. Their speed is a weapon they can really use, especially against the Devils. Time for some dramatic decisions. Rita and the leaders discuss some radical moves. She feels that perhaps Maya and Ruby coming more into the centre would give the Scorpions more options. She wants to know what the leadership group thinks.

Will Ruby and Maya move to onballer positions to provide more speed?
Go to page 93

OR

Will Coach Rita decide to leave things as they are?
Go to page 104

You decided that the umpire rules it as touched and calls it a behind.

It's a behind! Well, that was touch-and-go. Belle of the Devils is certainly a force to contend with. Hope the umpy got it right. Looks like she did but we have no video umpire at this level. Maybe a couple of the supporters could be stationed at each end of the ground to take videos of the action. Might help the umpires but probably takes too long.

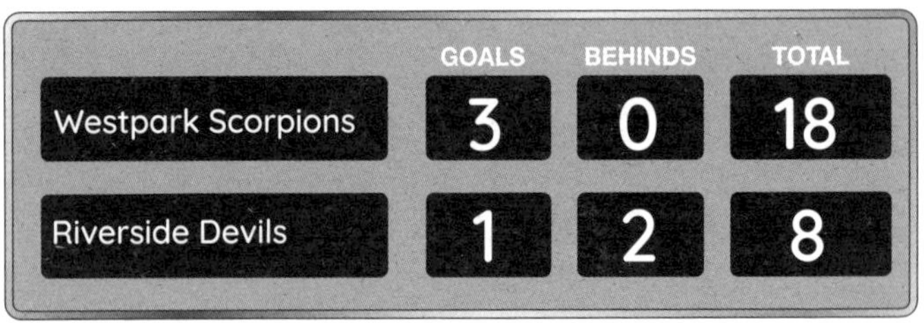

	GOALS	BEHINDS	TOTAL
Westpark Scorpions	3	0	18
Riverside Devils	1	2	8

Anyway, enough of this banter as we see Hannah giving the ball to Beth for the kick-out. Hannah obviously still not trusting herself at the moment. Probably should've taken the kick-out. Best thing to do once you've fallen off the horse is to get right back on.

Beth kicks long down the centre corridor and the ball runs free. A pack of players descend on the ball just as the siren sounds for half-time.

HALF-TIME

As the girls come into the rooms, Coach Rita pulls Hannah aside and tells her that just because she made a blue doesn't mean she's going to keep making mistakes.

'One of the tricks to playing footy, Hannah, is that as soon as you make an error you put it out of your mind and go even harder. The more you let it get into your head, the more bad things will happen.' Coach Rita gives Hannah a little hug which brings a smile to her face.

'C'mon, girls. Get those oranges into you and give yourselves a rest. And I've just been reminding Hannah that you can't afford to let mistakes ruin your whole game. It's only ONE mistake! Remember that.' To emphasise her point, Coach Rita punches her fist into her hand and repeats. 'It's only ONE mistake!! Now check your taping and rest up. Important quarter coming up.'

As the Scorpions prepare to run out for the third quarter, Zoe calls them into a group. Dylan tags along. He's like her shadow.

'We won back the lead so let's keep it going. The Devils are super strong so focus and pressure.'

The girls link arms as they listen to their captain.

'All hands in – Go Scorpions!!'

THIRD QUARTER

Both teams look as though the pressure of this game has taken it out of them as we start the third quarter. It is a riveting contest.

Devils' ruck Maggie belts the ball into the clear. To no one's advantage. Ava and Grace pounce and they're in contention with a number of Devils. Ball gets caught up in a tight pack. Outside runners waiting for it to come out. They're circling. Maybe Scorps don't have enough in-and-under players, which they'll need if they're going to beat the tough and experienced Devils. It's not coming out. Bodies falling over like tenpins. Then Talia comes in from nowhere. She's had a very good match. Playing her twelfth game. Slaps it out wide. Two players scramble for the ball. Zoe comes in to lend a hand and scoops it up, slick handball to Thao who backtracks and passes to a player running past. Goes wide but there's a free going to Devils.

Coach Rita might think about swinging a few changes. So it goes back the other way. Good battle, ball beats both of them. Throw-in.

Big ruck clash here. The intensity of the game has gone up dramatically. The ball keeps ping-ponging backwards and forwards between the two 50-metre arcs. Scorpions' mid, Emma, comes in from the side and delivers a massive bump that floors one of the Devils' forwards. She's down. Players come from everywhere. Her teammates gather around. She's not moving. Tries to get to her feet. No. Down on her hands and knees. Umpy might pull out her book. Is the Scorpions' Emma going to be reported? Maybe for that deliberate hard bump. Unduly rough play is my guess.

Meanwhile, a Devils player is helped off the ground by the Devils' medicos.

Dr Vanessa goes over to help check her out. It's doubtful that she'll make a return today.

Means one less on the bench for the Devils.

Does Emma get reported for unduly rough play?
Go to page 62

OR

Does the umpire decide not to report Emma?
Go to page 71

You decided that the umpire ruled it as a goal.

Goal to the Devils. To be honest, if it wasn't for the tough bullocking work by Belle that wouldn't have gone through. Seemed like half the Scorpions' team was in the goal square to stop that goal. Belle and her teammates are whooping it up while Holly and Matilda are still arguing the toss with the umpy, claiming they touched it. Zoe pulls Holly aside. We don't know what was said but it's had the desired effect. Matilda still looking grumpy. As the ball comes back for a new bounce, Andy the runner comes out to Matilda and it looks like she's coming off for a spell. Alexandra, one of the new Scorpions, runs out to take her place on the half-back line. Good coaching by Rita. No shame in Matilda coming off although her dad, Joe, doesn't look too happy but keeps it under control. A bit of time for Matilda to cool off.

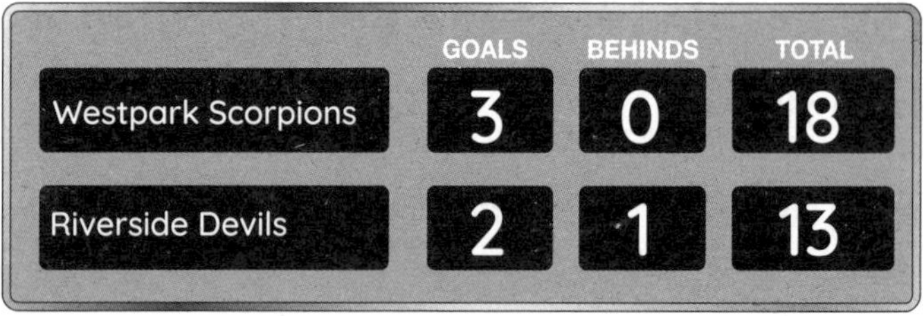

Big bounce and as it sails into the air, Heidi takes a run-up and taps it down to her mids who are waiting. But her perfect tap turns out to be not so perfect as Devils shark the tap-out and they're away, taking it through the centre. Scorpions will have to be strong in defence as Laini, who's bravely left her opposition, comes out and gathers at half-back. She's tackled but still manages to somehow get the ball to Maya who is under close attention. Scorps fighting hard here, but the Devils are clearly up for the fight. They wrestle the ball away and push it into their 50.

Ball still being fought over. Ball going nowhere. Then out comes new girl Alexandra. Nobody was keeping an eye on her. She's got a bit of speed. Scoops up the ball with one hand, arches her back.

Doesn't look like she's got passing it off on her mind. Just wants to get it up ground. Gets beyond 50 and boots the ball to the wing, where Grace and Ruby are waiting.

Grace charges at it. Devils come at them, with the Devils' centre doing all the tackling work. Ruby boots forward, Ava gets bundled out of it. Scorpions looking to get the ball out into the open to clear. Sophie takes it, passes to Zoe who gets it to Thao and kicks towards the Scorpions' 50 but now taken in defence by Devils' full-back. She's had eleven touches so far, and her input is still strong in this game. Now she looks to switch into the corridor and finds a Scorpion in the way.

Options in the 50, couple in space, once more into the Scorpions' 50. Zoe and Thao jostling for position. Finally somebody has got it. It's the Devils' defence again, working overtime. Their full-back is brimming with confidence. She runs and bounces and takes it out to the wing. Sophie slaps it back toward the Scorpions' 50 yet again where the ball tumbles forward but, yes you guessed it, the Devils' fullback once again is there in defence. Good work by her and back the play goes into the centre. Untidy footy on both sides.

Out on the wing again and Sophie handballs it down the line. Scorpions are having trouble in stringing a few possessions together. Margin sits at five points in favour of the Scorpions. Now Scorps' mid is having some influence as she gets a free for something. Not sure what that was for. Never mind, Talia happy to take the free.

Scorpions are desperate to increase their lead, and with so many forward incursions with no chocolates, their desperation grows. Talia kicks very long to their forward line where Zoe marks strongly. She read that well. Opportunity here. Forty-five out. Too far out for her to score. She dodges around her opponent on the mark and with no other option, goes for it. Lands and now Ivy, who has just come off the bench, leaps and brings it to ground. Still under her control. Tackled hard, breaks the tackle, takes a few steps, tackled again with the ball still in her grasp, falls over, not giving up that ball in her hands, on her knees, scrambles up, Devils' defender reaches out and takes her legs. Should've been called a trip, Ivy doesn't wait for the whistle, staggers, breaks clear and curls a snap. Goal! Brilliant. Did not give up for one second.

Broke three tackles plus what was most certainly a trip and goals. That'll go on her highlights reel. And there's the siren for half-time. Goes to show what second and third attempts can do. In this instance, a goal. Scorpions leave the field all hugging Ivy.

HALF-TIME

In the rooms the girls wolf down the oranges and glug down their water. Coach Rita talks to them while this is going on. She points out Ivy's desperation for that last goal.

Rita says, 'Girls, I know you've all put in and I'm proud of your efforts but I'm bringing up Ivy's play as an example of how important those one and two percenters are. She broke three tackles, was clearly tripped but didn't hesitate to wait for the umpire to blow her whistle and kept going which ended up in a goal. It's about sustaining the pressure and then still performing.'

Applause echoes in the rooms. Dr Vanessa checks some of the players for any signs of hamstring tightness, although that happens far less with girls this age.

Game's about to begin again. Leadership group of Zoe, Heidi and Beth get the girls around in a circle.

Beth speaks up: 'I know we're a couple of goals up but the worst thing we can do is to think we have it won. We're way more inexperienced than the Devils so they'll be thinking that's all we've got. We have to come out like we're starting the match all over again. Keep the pressure on them. All hands in. Scorpions!!'

Their yell reverberates as they run out onto the field again and the crowd claps and cheers, yelling encouragement: 'Go Scorps. You can do it! We're with you!'

You have to love a loud and positive group of supporters.

Centre bounce. Heidi takes it directly out of the air and boots quickly out towards Ruby. She collects off one bounce and puts out a strong arm to fend off her Devils opponent. Doesn't work. Ruby tries to slip by with some fancy footwork, Devils player reaches out to tackle but looks like she got Ruby around her neck. Looks like a high tackle.

Does the umpire see the high tackle and award a free to Ruby?
Go to page 78

OR

Does the umpire miss the high tackle on Ruby and call 'Play on'?
Go to page 85

You decided that the Devils player Belle was not shepherded and that Hannah's mark stands.

Hannah's mark stands. Oh boy. If that doesn't rile the Devils, nothing will. Although it was touch-and-go that Belle was shepherded out of play.

Hannah grins like a mullet and takes the ball. Takes a quick kick to the left pocket where Beth marks. She puts up her hand to tell her teammates to slow things down. Situations like that sometimes get the blood up and decisions are made hastily. Beth goes back to Hannah. Devils have picked up all their opposition and have shut down a Scorpions easy exit. Laini runs past Hannah who handballs to her, then it's back to Hannah again who does a lovely kick to the opposite corner. Matilda goes long down the line, trusting her players to contest the ball.

Mark by Heidi. What a mark! Great leverage off the opposition player. Just pushed off and launched. Stayed up there for a long time. Plucked it out of the air. Landed back on terra firma with a wallop. She gets up gingerly, feeling her right hip.

Heidi tries to take it into centre corridor. Bad kick due to that hip. Looking for Sophie. Gets wrapped up straightaway. There's a player down in trouble – we'll keep you posted. Bouncing ball. Maya and Ruby in hot pursuit. Maya gets there first and boots it into forward 50. Nobody there really. The kick had great penetration. Players rushing for the contest. Talia picks it up but tumbles over. Now there's heaps of players in there. Chance for a free kick but nothing doing. Ump not interested. Thought Grace had her head just about ripped off.

Devils' defenders are sticking to their defensive work. Devils' back Isla slices a kick to her teammate who decides to move it quickly. Kicks to a one-on-one. Zoe wrestles it away, handballs to Emma. Both teams in a bit of confusion. Not sure who's got it. Now Talia's got the ball and runs away from her own goal. Thirty metres out. Got herself into a worse position. Decides to keep running but doubles back and sees Ava way out on the other side. Turns and delivers a long field kick which falls neatly into Ava's hands. Ava keeps running, doesn't miss a beat with Devils hot on her heels. At the last minute, Ava sees the goals, must be 40 metres out, she goes for a long, long, long kick. Through it goes. That'll lift the Scorpions' spirits as half-time siren is sounded. What a kick!

	GOALS	BEHINDS	TOTAL
Westpark Scorpions	3	0	18
Riverside Devils	2	1	13

HALF-TIME

Lots of jubilation in the rooms after that goal but Anna gets the team back on song, telling the girls to get on with whatever they have to do. Taping, maybe a bit of liniment, water, oranges, and red snakes for a quick sugar hit. Just sitting down and getting their breath back.

Rita walks around the room, checking on her charges. She doesn't overdo her instructions. More that the team keeps on doing what it's doing. She reminds them that they have to get the ball moving forward at every opportunity. 'Keep the pressure on the opposition and let's use our speed and really make them run!'

Zoe, Beth and Heidi gather the girls in close around them. 'Okay, hands in!' they shout before they run back onto the field.

THIRD QUARTER

Devils emerge from their rooms with grit and determination on their faces. Let's see if they can turn that into goals.

Game underway and Devils snare the ball but are tackled immediately by Sophie. Dropping the ball! Sophie handballs to an outside running player who gets a kick away. Pressure is improving by the Scorpions' team.

There's a stoppage. Devils' players emerge with the pill and get a rushed kick into their forward line, but there's a turnover caused by Holly who wastes no time at all with a driving kick-out to the flank. Scorps are moving the ball fast. Comes to Alex who has just come onto the ground. She traps the ball. Spills free. Ruby kicks it off the ground. Devils have been spread too wide. There's loose Scorpions everywhere. Over to Heidi, who passes to Elly who snaps a goal!

	GOALS	BEHINDS	TOTAL
Westpark Scorpions	4	0	24
Riverside Devils	2	1	13

Scorpions' crowd has gone completely berserk. Matilda's dad could be heard a few kilometres away. There's a chant going up. Some supporters have brought along a drum and a trumpet. Don't know how musical it is but nobody seems to mind. It only abates when the game starts again.

Talia has come into the ruck, with Heidi going forward. That's a tick of confidence in the team by Rita.

Devils win the knock but are snared by Sophie who does a long handball to Grace, who does another long handball. Devils are in absolute disarray. Ball in the hands of Heidi who chips the ball to Emma who stops in her tracks and is going to go for goal. She's about 20 out on a 45-degree angle. Zoe tells her to settle and take her time. She seems to be working out whether she'll do a check side kick or a straight drop punt. The check side is often the chosen style these days and players practise it all the time.

Will Emma choose a check side kick?
Go to page 115

OR

Will Emma choose a drop punt?
Go to page 125

You decided that Emma is reported for unduly rough play.

Emma takes being reported badly. Her shoulders slump. She's gone over to the Devils' player Isla, who is being helped from the ground. Touches her arm to let her know she's sorry. Thank heavens there was no head knock, otherwise matters would be a lot worse at the Tribunal.

Emma's teammates come over to her to offer some sympathy. Clearly this is an accident. Emma's not known for dirty play but that bump was pretty hard and the Devils' player, Isla, went down like a sack of potatoes. She's on the bench now and at least is sitting upright. Their medico is checking her out and Dr Vanessa goes over to lend a hand. Family members run over to the Devils' bench to the injured Isla.

Coach Rita takes Emma off and brings on Alex. Time on the bench will help Emma compose herself. Meanwhile, the crowd is silent with concern.

Big amount of time gone. Ump blows her whistle and the game gets underway again. Devils attack. They've got some drive in their work now. Probably due to that knock on their teammate. Something like that can work both ways. Either knocks the stuffing out of a side or it can spur them on. In this case it seems to have worked to the Devils' advantage.

Contested ball. Umpire says, 'It's mine.'

Heidi and Devils' ruck Maggie face each other. Up they go. Nobody wins the contest. Devils there in numbers. Team's playing well but Holly wins the ball and does a wild kick which sails over the heads of everybody. Battle for the ball going on here but Devils' onballer Jo is taken high and she gets the free. Beautiful kick to their forward line, big pack forms with Devils' Belle, who takes three bites at the cherry but can't control it. Falls to the ground, staggers to her feet, surrounded on all sides, snares the ball and in the midst of all those players snaps a goal for the Devils. Great goal, Belle!

	GOALS	BEHINDS	TOTAL
Westpark Scorpions	3	0	18
Riverside Devils	2	2	14

So it's only four points between them. Scorpions had a comfortable lead which is fast eroding. Devils snapping at their heels. Scorpions encouraging each other as they head into the centre. They're a youngish team so let's see how they deal with this attack by the Devils.

Game underway. A perfect tap by the Devils directly into the hands of Jo, their small onballer who feeds it out with a slick handpass to her teammate, who dodges, runs, bounces the ball, keeps running, sees a forward who's out on her own. Escaped her opposition, Scorpions' Chandra.

Ball delivered perfectly to the forward who marks it, arms outstretched in front of her. Nobody within cooee of her so she wanders into the goal and puts it through. Another goal to the Devils which puts them in front for the first time.

Just as the siren heralds the end of the third quarter.

	GOALS	BEHINDS	TOTAL
Westpark Scorpions	3	0	18
Riverside Devils	3	2	20

THREE-QUARTER TIME

Scorpions head over to their huddle where Coach Rita is waiting. I'm sure she'll have words to say about not dropping their heads and keeping up the pressure they've had working for most of the game. Mind you, the incident with Emma plus having play stopped for so long didn't help the focus of the Scorpions' team.

Rita gathers the team in close around her. Simple messages from her. 'Focus. Concentrate. Don't get distracted by the supporters. Believe in yourself, your teammates and remember all the skills we learnt and practised over the long Covid break.'

Arms around each other, Rita says, 'Stay strong. Let's go!'

FINAL QUARTER

Scorpions' team emerge from their huddle with some purpose. They've obviously been affected by the bump and the reporting of Emma.

Emma too has been affected badly which we could see with her effort in those last minutes of the third quarter when Coach Rita allowed her back on. She was throwing herself into every contest but without much direction or thought. This can happen, particularly to an inexperienced team. Let's see if they can quell the Devils' momentum.

First minutes of the final quarter and Scorpions have worked the ball forward. A good sign. Poppy drives it forward but intercept mark taken by the Devils' back who was lurking in space. She gets it to a teammate who executes a perfect bump on her opponent, Ava, and takes a strong grab. Nothing on offer so she sells some candy and runs around Ava and switches play to the other side where a Devil collects the ball.

Doesn't play on. Taking her time with a short kick which comes off. Now the Scorpions are flooding the back line. Devil does a very long handpass which doesn't quite work. Laini of the Scorpions has cut off that avenue and a pack forms.

Devils' mid Jo escapes but is now surrounded by opposition. Scorps have taken to heart the message that they have to stop the momentum, the drive coming from the Devils.

Play happening around the Devils half-back zone. Scrappy play. Almost holding the ball there. Ball comes out, Devils' onballers extract it again and now they're away! Not much up forward for them.

Devils' Jo kicks, big kick more in hope but it goes over the line and out on the full. Hannah takes the free but does a sneaky underground handball to Beth who is caught by three Devils and is ground into the turf.

Ball comes free, Devils' player pounces and sees a chance in the forward zone and sends it there where it's marked by Belle in a jumble of players. Twenty out, 45 degrees.

Siren sounds for the end of the game. Belle takes her shot, ball curves, she's kicked right to left. Looks like it's missing. But no, it sneaks through for a goal! And the Devils win by a margin of eight points.

	GOALS	BEHINDS	TOTAL
Westpark Scorpions	3	0	18
Riverside Devils	4	2	26

Poor Scorpions. After leading for most of the day, they've blown their chance of a gutsy victory. Certainly not humiliated but they'll have something to think about as they head off to the rooms.

A big lesson given to the Scorpions.

Devils were strong and disciplined today.

You decided that the umpire doesn't report Emma.

No, the umpy didn't see it as rough play. Just a tough bump which nevertheless sees Isla, one of the best Devils players, off the ground. Not sure if she'll be back on.

In fact, Emma now looks as though she's in trouble. She's limping pretty badly. Didn't see anything there. Maybe an old injury. She's had some problem with her calf muscle before.

Andy's out there but Emma waves him away and is walking okay now. Meanwhile, the ball gets thrown up. Beautiful tap by Heidi to Sophie and she gets a big kick away. Pack forms and ball comes to ground. Ruby is in and under. She gets it to Scorpions' outside runners. Handball to Thao who kicks wildly but it lands 20 metres out from goal. Bit of luck there. Again, Ruby is in there and once more gets it out with a desperate handball. Comes to Zoe who's facing away from goal but kicks it over her shoulder – and there's a goal for the highlights reel!!

	GOALS	BEHINDS	TOTAL
Westpark Scorpions	4	0	24
Riverside Devils	1	2	8

Scorpions crowd goes wild. Matilda's father Joe is banging his BBQ tongs on the table as well as adding his familiar booming voice to the cheering. Scorpions are now clearly in command.

Siren sounds to end the third quarter.

THREE-QUARTER TIME

Dr Vanessa and Anna immediately go over to Emma, who lies down while they go to work on her sore calf muscle. She tells them that she's okay but they say she needs attention. Rita checks with them to see if Emma is okay to get back on the ground. Thumbs up from Dr Vanessa.

Coach Rita now addresses her girls and tells them that she wants to see more of the type of play that she's seen in the last ten minutes.

'We're sixteen points up which is nothing for the Devils to deal with. They can score quickly and that's what their coach will be saying to them right now. Our defence will have to be at the top of their game.

'Hands in. SCORPIONS!!'

FINAL QUARTER

Margin, sixteen points in favour of the Scorpions. We're about to see what stuff the Scorpions are made of. That last goal by Zoe was fantastic and is bound to really raise their spirits.

And we're away in this final quarter. This game has met all our expectations. For a while there we thought the Devils were about to run away with it but the Scorpions, led very well by their leadership group, have held firm.

Sophie has taken it out of the centre and doesn't she love to run. Dodges, weaves around two opponents, decides to keep on running. Looking for something up forward. Now her teammates are running forward to give her something to kick to. Devils on her tail but Sophie gets a kick away, but goes into space where there's a stoppage. Ball-up. Away again. Crunching tackle by Devils, causes a turnover. Turnover is short-lived when Grace gets a loose ball and puts it back towards the Scorpions' 50 with a long kick. Pressure coming from both sides.

Intensity going through the roof. Devils' defence working well. Now Devils back line player Isla, who's recovered from that bump, is back on the ground and is in the thick of it again. She twists out of trouble, gets boot to ball but it sails over the line and out of bounds on the full.

Thao takes the free. She's hardly put a foot wrong all day. It's still in the Scorpions' forward pocket. Scorpions collect and try a chip kick but good smother by the Devils. Loose ball. Both sides fighting for the ball like there's no tomorrow.

Was that a dangerous tackle by the Devils? No. Scorps' player had her arms free. No room to move out there but Ruby bursts out of the pack and handballs wide, over her head. Devils' back Isla slips over at a critical time. Ball's going every which way.

Getting close to full-time. Good trap by Talia. Minutes ticking by. Ball drifting away from Scorpions' goal. Tap into clear space and Poppy picks up the ball with one hand – don't see that too often these days – straightens up and gets it back to Talia. She works the angle brilliantly. So calm in that situation.

Now Talia does a look-away handpass to Thao who snaps from 20 out and … and wait for it. I think it's a goal. Yes, it's a goal to the Scorpions!

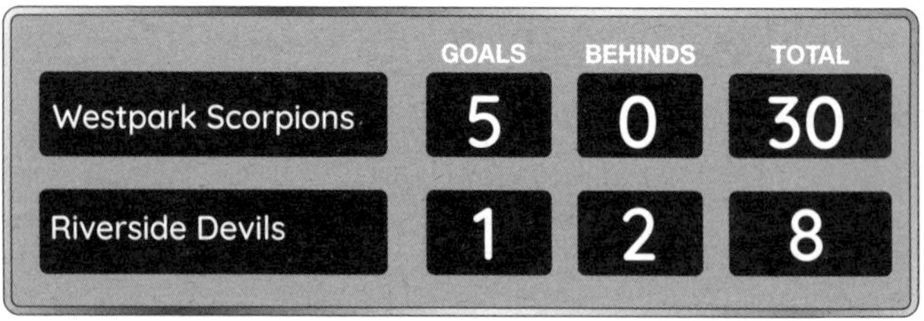

	GOALS	BEHINDS	TOTAL
Westpark Scorpions	5	0	30
Riverside Devils	1	2	8

Can you believe it?! And to put the cherry on top, there's the siren. Scorpions win in a landslide.

If there was a roof above this oval, it would've lifted off with the cheering that erupted. I'd say the Scorpions' Under 14s have arrived. Well and truly.

Scorpions held Devils goalless for most of the game. WOW. Scorpions outplay the super-strong Devils.

Coach Rita is out there giving the girls a hug as they walk off. She knows, even if her team doesn't, what a victory this has been.

Scorpions' parents and all supporters clap and applaud loudly as their team leaves the ground.

You decided that Ruby gets a free kick for a high tackle.

Free kick to Ruby. She certainly stands out today with her tough play. Ruby feeling her neck. Good that the umpire saw that, although not that hard to see. In fact, Ruby nearly had her head ripped off. No intention there but nevertheless Ruby is not feeling too good. Umpire asks her if she's able to take the kick. Ruby answers by handballing to Beth who doesn't connect too well with the footy and floats it toward the pocket.

Good mark taken by Sophie who, believe it or not, does a spiral torpedo to the Scorpions' goal square. Monstrous kick and then rolled forever. Rarely seen these days but Sophie's kick certainly covered some territory.

Ball in dispute in the goal square. Alex battling Devils' defence but can't get it out. Mopped up by Devils' backs, who get it out to Jo who's waiting for it.

Decides on going long and wide and on to her teammate, but she misses the target and there's a boundary throw-in.

Scores are 24 to 13 in favour of the Scorpions who have been fantastic today. A few glitches here and there but a much-improved side since last time when they could play every week. Umpire pulls out a free for a ruck infringement. Goes to Scorpions' Maya who has taken over ruck work and given Heidi a rest in the forward pocket. Maya pops it up to the hot spot, Heidi is there – so are Ivy and Poppy. Scorpions are rotating their players frequently. Ava is front and centre. Gets it. Feeds it out but it's forced over by the Devils for a rushed behind to the Scorpions. Siren sounds for the end of the third quarter.

	GOALS	BEHINDS	TOTAL
Westpark Scorpions	4	1	25
Riverside Devils	2	1	13

THREE-QUARTER TIME

It's three-quarter time here at this big game between the Westpark Scorpions and the Riverside Devils. Both sides head off to their groups. Devils are gathered around their coach who seems to be reading the riot act to them. Devils held scoreless that quarter. Love to hear what she's saying. Probably telling them that it's no good to be kicking long to their 50 and hoping that someone will mark it, which is what they've been doing for much of their game. It'll be a matter of getting the Devils girls to lower their eyes and look for a target.

Meanwhile, Rita is very happy with the energy and effort of her Scorpions team. Last quarter coming up.

FINAL QUARTER

Devils are not done yet. There's been a switch on. Devils have moved their centre into their forward line, as if Belle needed help!

Good throw up. Devils' onballer, Jo, in the clear, wonderful pick up by their ruck, Maggie, who bangs it quickly forward but nobody can take it clearly.

Pack forms, there's bodies falling everywhere. Scorpions know the Devils are desperate. Devils out to their forward pocket player who gets handball out to another forward standing all alone 30 metres out. She puts it to goals but just misses. One behind! That's at least better work by the Devils.

	GOALS	BEHINDS	TOTAL
Westpark Scorpions	4	1	25
Riverside Devils	2	2	14

Kick in by Laini but bad error. Didn't see Devils' forward, Belle, who was too close for that kind of kick to work. Devils player comes in and takes the mark from that dreadful kick. Bad kick-out and bad choice but clever little mark to Devils who will now make Scorpions pay. Right through the middle it goes. Goal!

	GOALS	BEHINDS	TOTAL
Westpark Scorpions	4	1	25
Riverside Devils	3	2	20

Now it's on for young and old with not long to go. The margin is only five points in favour of the Scorpions.

Game starts and the Scorpions look a little bewildered. They've had the game under their control for much of the match.

Andy, the runner, is working overtime, taking messages out to several of the players. Main message you can guess. Back to basics and stop panicking.

Heidi back in the ruck. She's worked hard all day but has been missing in the last ten minutes.

Ball comes to ground. Scorpions are attacking the ball with strength. Ava looks like she's making a getaway but is nailed by a Devils' player.

Ball still not coming out. Great numbers around the ball. Both sides know the outcome is hanging in the balance.

Devils' ruck Maggie muscles her way through. Now they've got it and Devils have to GO! That's a good hit up to her teammate in the centre corridor. She's in a hurry.

Not long to go now. Ball lands on the ground. Scorps kick at it. With no effect. A pack of players are after the elusive pill. Whistle blows. Umpire has pulled out a free kick to who? It's the Devils' forward, Belle. It's for kicking in danger. Siren sounds. Devils back from the brink. This is a gettable goal. Twenty out and a very slight angle. Belle takes her time. Pulls up her socks. Tucks her mouthguard in one. Scorpions on the mark jumping up and down. Belle begins her run-up. Measured kick.

Goal to Devils. They've pulled the win out of the fire. Scorpions led most of the day. Might be a hard lesson for the young team.

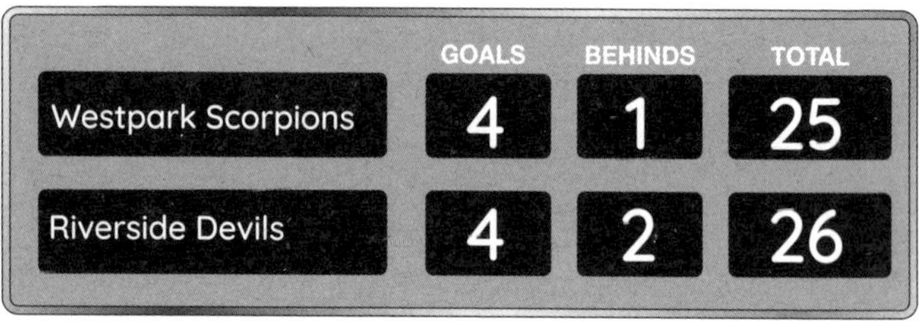

	GOALS	BEHINDS	TOTAL
Westpark Scorpions	4	1	25
Riverside Devils	4	2	26

Devils go wild. Scorpions are in disbelief. A few tears here and there as they walk slowly off the ground with their supporters giving them appreciative applause and pats on the back as they head into their rooms. Beaten by one point. Now that's going to be a bitter pill for the Scorpions to swallow.

You decided that the Umpire doesn't see the high tackle and calls 'Play on'.

Umpire says the tackle was fine. All okay. Well, the crowd has reacted to that call. Umpire calls, 'Play on.' Even some of the Devils stopped play because of that tackle. Oh well, them's the breaks. Ruby nearly had her head taken off. She's gesticulating to the umpire but she better get on with it because the game has gone on.

And on it goes. That call has thrown things into confusion. Scorpions were nicely set up behind the ball but now they're like chooks with their heads cut off. Leadership group issuing instructions left, right and centre. Andy the runner is out there, specifically talking to the defence.

Devils' forwards are throwing themselves into the battle. Tug of Holly's arm should have been a Scorpion free but nothing doing.

‘Play on’ is the call. Devils’ Jo knocks the ball clear. Huge chance here. The Devils will have to pull something out of the bag. Belle hovering. Somehow grabs the ball, but she fumbles due to intense pressure. Can’t get away and is wrapped up.

The ball has been in the Devils’ forward zone forever but they don’t seem to be able to take advantage of the confusion. Lots of contested play out at the 50-metre line. Devils get it out and manage a short chip pass to their forward but intercepted by Chandra who takes a very strong mark. It’s like she has superglue on her hands today. Looks up for some leads. Nothing on offer so decides to sell some candy and runs around Devil on her mark and takes off. Wow, she’s got some speed. Used to be in love with soccer but now in love with Aussie Rules.

Chandra’s footwork attests to her soccer background. She’s still going.

Dodges another. Bounces once. Twice. Through the centre she goes.

Another bounce and no Devil can catch her. This is incredible.

Reaches 40 metres out. Now 30. She's run all the way from the Devils' defence to here. Lines up and bang! Whoa. Through the big sticks and it's a sausage roll! Mobbed by her teammates.

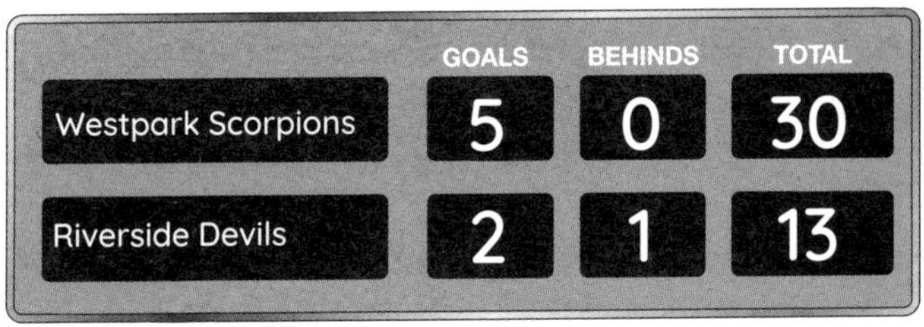

Car horns tooting. Yelling. Applause. Not quite like the MCG but it'll do.

Chandra will never forget that. Players head back to the centre, but as the ball is thrown up, siren sounds for the end of the third quarter.

THREE-QUARTER TIME

The coach reminds the girls that it's their intensity that's got them to this spot. Anna is reminding some of the team to rehydrate and Dylan is having a good time running around handing out water bottles. Dr Vanessa checks out Ruby after that tackle. All okay. She also checks out some of the defence six for any head knocks. Sometimes difficult to see when it happens and sometimes the girls don't want to tell anybody for fear of going off and having a concussion test. Not a good idea but shows how determined this team is.

Zoe, Heidi and Beth urge their teammates to focus and apply pressure on their opponents.

'Hands in. GO SCORPIONS!'

FINAL QUARTER

Close to a three-goal Scorpions lead. Scorpions will have to keep up the pressure because the Devils are sure to come out ready to flex their muscles. And off we go again.

Scorps are not showing any signs of slackening off the pace. But within one minute the Devils have booted long and tough into their forward zone where it's gathered by one of their onballers who does a check side snap, but it's only one behind. That kind of score is not going to bring the Devils back into the game.

	GOALS	BEHINDS	TOTAL
Westpark Scorpions	5	0	30
Riverside Devils	2	2	14

Hannah has regained some confidence after a few earlier errors and completes a perfect kick-out, which goes out onto the flank, where Matilda collects the ball after one bounce and switches play into the corridor where Sophie is all alone. Goes to take off but is nailed by a Devil, but still she manages to not drop the ball and gets a kick away as she slides along the turf. It seems like the Scorpions want the ball more than the Devils.

Players from both sides are battling for the ball. They must be weary by now but Scorps in particular have found another gear.

Devils' older players are trying to go up a notch and take charge of the game. Their centre has just taken another possession, adding another one to her tally. She gets it going back the other way with a little run of her own but is tackled by two Scorpions, Holly and Beth.

Dropping the ball. Beth gets the free and takes off, going sideways to Sophie who's been screaming for the ball. Starts to go but decides to hold things up to give her teammates a chance to run forward.

Does a chip kick to Grace who also waits. They're using this to eat up some time. Good idea usually but the Devils only need one Scorpions slip-up and they'll make the Scorpions pay.

Now Grace has stopped mucking around and goes for a monster kick which sails over the heads of a pack of players and is taken by Alex with a one-handed mark. A bit of a juggle but she's got it.

She's indicated to the ump that she's going for goal. Takes the full 30 seconds. Might be beyond her capabilities. Big kick, big kick. Nothing wrong with that and it might make the distance but it's going slightly offline. Almost there. Out of the blue Talia soars in from the side and marks on the behind post. What a mark!! It's going to be a check side kick. But before she gets to do that, the siren goes. There's muted celebrations by the Scorpions but they all settle down for Talia to take the shot. Umpire tells her it'll have to be a drop punt because she isn't allowed to go off her line. Talia goes back. You could hear a pin drop. Taking her time. Through it goes!!! And now she's mobbed and carried off the ground. What a victory. Scorpions have humiliated the powerful and experienced Devils. Their speed and focus really ripped apart that super strong Devils team. Kept them under the pump all day.

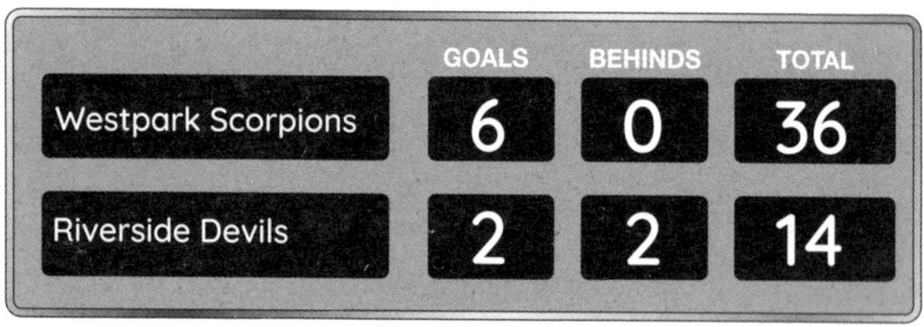

	GOALS	BEHINDS	TOTAL
Westpark Scorpions	6	0	36
Riverside Devils	2	2	14

With extraordinary accuracy the Scorpions have won by 22 points. Great effort.

HALF-TIME

You decided that Ruby and Maya move to onballer positions to provide more speed.

Coach Rita tells the team that those two will be starting in the Centre and that every opportunity for moving the ball quickly should be taken.

‘Sure, we’ll make mistakes but I don’t want that to stop you from being daring. It’s our being prepared to take a few chances that’s got us to here. If there’s a chance to go through the centre corridor, then do it. Let’s really use our speed. All hands in. Scorpions!!’

Heidi, Beth and Zoe lead the girls back onto the ground.

THIRD QUARTER

Off we go into this enthralling contest. A five-point game. As was said by the great coach David Parkin, this quarter is often known as 'the premiership quarter'. It's make or break for the Scorpions.

There's been a dramatic change. Maya and Ruby have moved to the centre. We've heard that these two are the fastest in the team. Maya apparently was into athletics at school and is certainly fleet of foot. So that's what we can expect – some fast footwork. It's a big call so we'll see what happens.

Ball goes up and Heidi reaches for the clouds. A perfect tap but sharked by the Devils who have their own speedsters as well. Their outside runners have moved into top gear. They know that this young team they're up against are no easy beats.

Devils are spreading now. They seem to have loose players everywhere. Devils forwards calling for the ball. Screaming for the ball.

Bad field kick giving the Scorpions a chance here. But bad fumble by Holly and now the Devils' Jo seizes the opportunity.

She's off, eluding grasping hands. Does a fancy spin out of trouble but is confronted by Ruby who has got her in a vice-like grip and brings her to ground.

Whoomph! That would've hurt. Taken the wind out of the Devil.

Ruby, who laid that tackle, obviously remembers Rita's words.

Doesn't wait around and short passes to Maya who looks up and finds nothing there. Goes sideways, giving her teammates time to run into space.

Some of these girls have great engines. Maya and Ruby are not only fast on their feet, but Maya also has explosive speed.

Chip pass by Maya, then it's two Scorps on one Devil. Scorpions still getting the ball. In the hands of Ruby, who's attacked by Devil onballer Jo. She handballs on to Maya who is under the pump. She goes back to Ruby, the two girls keep moving the ball forward.

Ruby grabbed but manages to put it onto – guess who? – Maya, who has kept running, reaches 40, 30, 25. This is a big kick, she decides to go for it herself and strikes the ball. Going, going, going. Through! A spectacular goal.

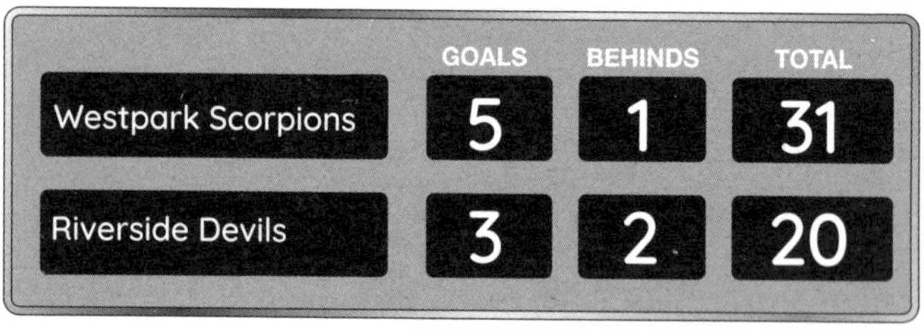

	GOALS	BEHINDS	TOTAL
Westpark Scorpions	5	1	31
Riverside Devils	3	2	20

Siren sounds for the end of the quarter. Devils held goalless!

The Maya and Ruby move has paid off, so far at any rate.

THREE-QUARTER TIME

Girls move into their different groups. Forwards, mids and backs.

Anna moves around making sure they rehydrate. Dr Vanessa talks to a few girls who have pulled up a bit sore. One of the girls, Laini, was cramping up in the last few minutes of that quarter. She's put in a lot of work.

Coach Rita goes to each group with specific instructions. She's been delighted by that last goal but knows the Devils will be onto it. She doesn't want the rest of the team to simply rely on those two girls.

Andy the runner chips in saying that if he was the Devils' coach he'd be tagging Maya and Ruby. Rita reminds the girls that the Devils are a really experienced team and will come back hard in the last quarter.

She calls the team into a tight group.

'Hands in. Go Scorpions!!!' resounds across the ground as the siren sounds to start the final quarter.

FINAL QUARTER

And we're away. Devils have been revved up by a fiery three-quarter time speech from their coach. And their first few moments demonstrated that.

Sure enough, they've put their taggers onto Ruby and Maya. The Devils don't want to see that combo dominate play in the last quarter.

Ball-up again and now it's over the line and out of bounds. Throw-in and tap leads to a pack forming. Heidi has got it. She'll have to be careful here. Looks like she dragged it back in.

Umpire having a close look. Yes, she's gone! Free kick to the Devils who waste no time in driving it into their forward 50. Nobody's ball. Devils get it out and their forward snaps and it goes through for . . . a behind.

	GOALS	BEHINDS	TOTAL
Westpark Scorpions	5	1	31
Riverside Devils	3	3	21

Ten points the difference in favour of the Scorpions. Still a close game.

Hannah delivers to Beth, waiting in the back pocket. She executes a dangerous kick to Holly in front of the Devils' goal, but Holly takes a strong grab.

Would've been ugly if that didn't come off. Sees Ruby off to her right and again a perfect field kick to her. Ruby takes off, shakes her tag and goes back into the centre again.

Maya takes off but is run down by Devils. Still manages to get the ball away with a side kick at the last minute which results in a milling pack.

Zoe and Thao are at it, but Zoe pokes it over the top. Alex defends and kicks it back to where it came from.

Bit of a kick to kick going on here.

Now in the middle of the ground, Grace gathers with one hand, beautiful. Like poetry in motion. Don't see much of that these days, and she takes off. Three Devils players are hot on her hammer. They better get her here because a certain goal is coming up. Hands outstretched and Devils' back Isla has got her! Great tackle.

Ball spills free and Devils defend with a short kick to the defensive 50-metre arc. Great one percenter, that tackle by the way. Can make or break a game.

Devils' mid decides to not go back into the centre but goes to outer wing where it's a contest between two players. Ivy and the Devils' brilliant onballer Jo. Comes down to the ground. Ivy somehow collects the leather and gets it to Emma who has arrived in the nick of time. She goes for a run. Devils' speedster is on her tail but there's Ruby running into the clear.

Emma foot passes to Ruby who reaches 30, difficult angle, but handballs over the top of Devils' defender to Alex who turns around and kicks a simple goal.

	GOALS	BEHINDS	TOTAL
Westpark Scorpions	6	1	37
Riverside Devils	3	3	21

Big celebrations. Is there time left for the Devils to improve their score? Must be only minutes left. Ruck battle but umpy calls for the ball.

Ball-up, but again that ball is going nowhere. Ball-up again and Heidi slaps the ball out to Thao who gets it hurriedly onto her boot where it lands in the very safe hands of Zoe.

Andy is out there letting the Scorpions know how much time's left. Zoe plays it safe and kicks backwards to Chandra. She takes her time. Scorps won't need to make a mistake here.

Chandra sees Holly who marks safely.

Umpire calls, 'Not fifteen!'

Holly is descended upon by Devils. But the siren goes signalling the end of the game. And the Scorpions' Under 14 girls' team run to each other. A Scorpion win!

A big win against a really strong and experienced Devils outfit.

The leadership group gathers the Scorpions together and they walk off the ground as one, as their supporters show their appreciation for such a strong victory.

HALF-TIME

You decided that Coach Rita decides to leave things as they are.

After chatting with the leadership group and Anna, Rita decides against bringing both girls into the centre. She thinks it might make the side a bit unbalanced. Rita finishes her half-time instructions to the girls. 'Hands in. GO SCORPIONS!'

Zoe urges her teammates to focus and apply pressure on their opponents as she leads the team onto the ground for the premiership quarter.

THIRD QUARTER

So, it's into the third quarter with the Scorpions up by five points. It is still anybody's game. Both sides lacking accuracy with a lot of their kicking at times.

We begin again and Devils shark the ball and away she goes. But Matilda is in the way and gets it back. Handball went behind her teammate. But she's somehow got it back in her hands and keeps going. Runs to 30 out. Runs to 25. Over to Grace and goal to the Scorpions. Great start! What a wonderful team goal.

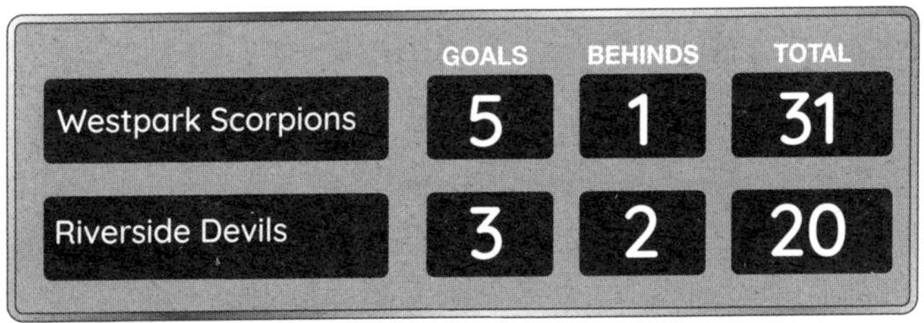

	GOALS	BEHINDS	TOTAL
Westpark Scorpions	5	1	31
Riverside Devils	3	2	20

When the Scorpions get it into space they're hard to stop. They can really use that pace they have. Better than level-pegging now with the ball back to the centre.

This time the tap is taken by the Scorps' Emma who kicks to space. Touched off the boot. Umpy yells, 'Play on.' Don't think anybody heard that. Umpire still yelling, 'Touched!' Comes down to a pack of players, with Sophie claiming the mark but hasn't heard the 'play on' so it's a ball-up. Devils' onballer Jo does a smart piece of roving, over to her running partner, long handball to Belle who snaps a very clever goal.

Neither team can seem to get a clear break on the scoreboard. But now it's the Devils less than a goal behind.

	GOALS	BEHINDS	TOTAL
Westpark Scorpions	5	1	31
Riverside Devils	4	2	26

You get the feeling that if the Devils get the next goal, they'll run away with the game. Both sides in the next few minutes will be looking for turnovers. Scorpions just haven't got enough of the footy. Mistakes by either side and the other will make them pay.

Game continues on the far side of the ground. Scorpions' Grace has been penalised for not throwing the ball back quickly enough to the Devils' player. Not sure whether that was the case. Beth and Heidi are calling on teammates to get into right positions. Scorpions need strong defence. Devils go for a long bomb into their forward line. Only reaches the 50. Tackle account is huge. Belle has plonked herself deep in the goal square. Devils kick is misdirected and goes over the line.

Enthralling and tactical game. Throw-in but Heidi slips over. Ball going nowhere. Ball-up. Ball comes out and Ruby gets a quick kick in and goes high down the line. Thao goes to ground. Enter Elly who keeps getting better and better. Elly controls the ball well and kicks past the opposition. Maggie, the Devils' ruck with a good run gets the mark. Play on. Long and strong. But Devils can't control it. Talia emerges and does a long bomb back towards Scorps' goal. It's in the pocket. Ava evades two, wheels around and sends it on its way. It's curling, curling, curling curls it through.

	GOALS	BEHINDS	TOTAL
Westpark Scorpions	6	1	37
Riverside Devils	4	2	26

What a moment for Ava. Scorpions ahead by eleven points as the siren sounds for Three-Quarter time.

THREE-QUARTER TIME

Scorps gather in the middle of the ground. Coach Rita is totally impressed with the Scorpions' effort in that quarter and now taking a handy lead in the last quarter. She congratulates her team on holding their nerve and playing well under pressure. A simple message from the coach: focus, pressure, commitment. The girls run to their positions to start the final quarter.

FINAL QUARTER

Last fling at the big dance. Who's going to outlast the other? More to the point, who's going to kick the all-important goals? Ball-up and big thump by Maggie towards the Devils' 50 arc.

Bursting out of the 50, it's Devils' mid Jo with a big kick. Belle marks, turns and gets it away. Ball bounces perfectly. But there's enough pressure to bring the ball to ground. In the forward zone for the Devils.

Momentum surges continue. Maggie breaks clear and is hunted down. Devils player gets the ball again but blazes away. Comes to nothing.

Pack forms, stopping game. Ball-up. Heidi handballs but straight into the hands of the opposition who hacks the ball into space. Fans give her warm applause. Chance here for Chandra charging through the corridor but Devils gun forward Belle marks in front of her. Belle spins around, sidesteps Chandra, takes a bounce and then launches a monster kick and scores a goal. Devils crowd jump to their feet! Huge Devils goal. Must've been 40 at least.

This is a high-energy game. Time's becoming an issue. Less than a goal between the teams. Nail-biting finish.

Ball-up. A scramble of players and ball surges forward for the Devils. Important hands by Matilda. All players, miss it. Beth breaks away and kicks long through the centre. Another pack forms and ball surges forward. Grace snaps but falls into the hands of the Devils' defender, Isla. They've got three or four big players down there. Smalls have to get to the contest. Front and centre.

Both teams are battling away. Heidi doing what she does so well. Gets down low and knocks it into the path of Grace, but is brought down just as quickly. It's a tackle fest.

Another ball-up. How many is that? We've lost count. After to-ing and fro-ing, ball once again booted into the Devils' forward zone. Holly's got it. Poor pass by Holly sees Belle intercept and dribble the ball towards the goals. It's on target but a diving lunge by Holly knocks it through for a behind. Devils score a behind.

	GOALS	BEHINDS	TOTAL
Westpark Scorpions	6	1	37
Riverside Devils	5	3	33

Laini kicks it out to Hannah who paddles the ball in front of her. Still going. Gathers. Loses it but still in her control. Gathers and now she's off! Twisting, stops, manages to get space then gets it out of there but to no one in particular. Doesn't matter because Poppy, who has read the play beautifully, collects and goes for a run. There's only a little time to go with the Devils four points behind.

There's a hurried kick to Scorps' forward line. Scorpions are hard at the contest. That's the way they like to play. Numbers are even around the ball. Poppy is burrowing in and emerges. Gets free. Runs around and kicks a short ball across the face of goal. Ivy hacks it out of mid-air. It's a goal! A much-needed goal and only seconds left.

	GOALS	BEHINDS	TOTAL
Westpark Scorpions	7	1	43
Riverside Devils	5	3	33

Game should be safe now with a ten-point lead to the Scorpions. And siren sounds just as the ball is taken back to the centre.

Huge celebrations. Whistling. Horns tooting. Somebody's banging a drum. Scorpions girls besiege Ivy, the kicker of that goal.

Scorpions win a heart-stopper! By ten points! How on earth did they do that?

As a group they walk off the ground proudly led by Ivy.

You decided that Emma chooses a check side kick.

Emma looks at the goals. She checks how far out she is. Drop punt would be her usual choice but by the way she's holding the ball, it looks like a check side. She has practised this a lot over lockdown and believes in herself but still feels super nervous. Goes back. Mouth guard in her sock. Crowd is hushed. She comes in on an angle and swings her right foot across her body. It curls, it needs to curl more than that. At the last minute, the ball curves dramatically and goes through. Another goal. Emma punches the air with sheer joy!

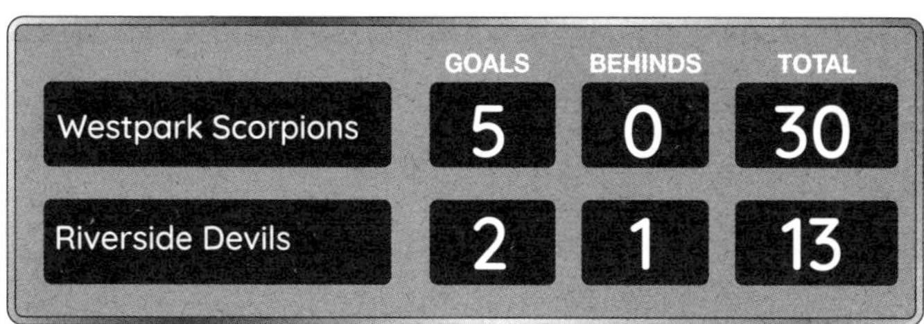

	GOALS	BEHINDS	TOTAL
Westpark Scorpions	5	0	30
Riverside Devils	2	1	13

Scorpions' crowd don't know what to do with themselves. They thought they might have a chance against the Devils but to be three goals ahead at this stage of the game is beyond their wildest dreams. Not sure, but I think the ground might be shaking with the roar from the crowd. Devils crowd can't quite believe it and are silenced by the scoreboard.

Not only was it a perfectly executed kick, but the Scorpions so far have kicked extremely accurately. Check side kicks, often called around-the-corner, snaps or bananas, don't always come off. Players also try them when they're too far out. But Emma thought it through. Great effort!

Anyway, back to the game.

Ball in the middle. Ball-up. Devils are throwing themselves into the contest. They're worried, which sometimes doesn't produce the best play. Frenzied attack on the ball and exactly what I was saying. An obvious free. The Devils crowd thinks the Scorpions' Sophie dropped her shoulder to get 'around the neck' but the free was definitely there. Sophie drives it into the Scorpions' forward line again. Strong mark by Alex but the siren goes for the end of the quarter and she's too far out to take a shot. Throws the ball to the umpire and the two teams go to opposite ends of the ground where their coaches and assistants are waiting for them.

THREE-QUARTER TIME

Dr Vanessa goes to a few girls to check them out. She also talks to Sophie who got the free in the middle for 'around the neck'. It was a pretty vicious tackle that pulled Sophie's head back. Apparently she's okay. Just a bit sore.

Rita tells the girls, 'Yes, you've played well and worked together as a team but the Devils will be hurting and the last thing they want is to be beaten by you lot. They're very experienced and have been a solid team for a few years before the pandemic. They'll want to come at you. They'll want that first goal to make you panic and lift their spirits. Keep doing what you're doing. No fancy stuff. Don't be afraid to work the ball forward and use your speed. If you make a mistake, keep your head up and make up for it. You're an amazing bunch of footy players and the crowd is behind you.

'All hands in. Scorpions!' Heidi, Beth and Zoe lead the team into position.

FINAL QUARTER

Can the Scorpions' Under 14 girls hang on? The Devils are a tenacious lot with loads of experience. They're three goals down with only one quarter to go. They won't have given up yet, even after being held goalless for two quarters!

It's on again and Devils are showing they mean business.

Ball-up and Devils' midfielder Jo sharks it. A good handpass off. Over the top. Devils show a little bit of run. Scorpions have been opened up here. Devils takes the grab. Gets up quickly. Short kick into the forward pocket and Belle collects and takes a hurried shot. It's too short but the ball bounces and eludes outstretched hands, and through it goes. Goal! Wow, what a way to start the final quarter. And the Devils' crowd goes berserk. It's been a while since the Devils fans had anything to cheer about.

	GOALS	BEHINDS	TOTAL
Westpark Scorpions	5	0	30
Riverside Devils	3	1	19

A few Scorpions' heads drop. Zoe and the leadership group won't stand for that. They run to the centre, urging their teammates on. Poppy and Alexandra have come off the interchange again and this time gone down back. Rita must think they've got the grunt to defend strongly.

Bounce in the centre. Bad bounce and it's brought back for a ball-up. Brave work there by Sophie getting in and under. Takes a pounding but she somehow gets it out. She's got courage under fire. Ruby gets a quick kick out to the flank where there's a race for the ball. Devils' player collects but she is taken over the line by Ava who dumps her on the ground just for good measure. I think the Scorpions are showing that they're up for the fight.

There's about another ten minutes for this story to unfold. Scorpions still with an eleven-point lead. Can they deal with these champions? That's the question.

Game starts again in the middle. Pack scrabbling for the ball. Getting to be an untidy game as both sides throw everything they've got. Sophie got possession with Devils attacking but she won't be intimidated. And she's got tons of speed. There she goes with first possession with a long kick but it comes to nothing. Thrown in. Up goes Heidi with a tap over the back to Elly who immediately weaves through traffic and gets it over to Emma who's been calling for it.

Into the centre corridor. Struggle between two players. Talia in there. Can she get it moving forward? Talia trying to get boot to ball. But Devils' mid Jo comes in from the side, gathers it and gets it out of the danger zone.

Important win for Devils with the crowd screaming Devils pass it to a player in support. And now it's away and up on the wing. Beautiful and timely intercept mark by Poppy who wastes no time at all and goes for a big boot. It's Grace who takes an uncontested mark against a rabble of a Devils' defence. Moves it quickly. Zoe marks in space.

Twenty out. No angle to speak of. Tucks her mouthguard into her socks. Flicks the ball around in her hands. Takes the kick and right through the hey-diddle-diddle. Players come from everywhere. Now that's a captain's mark and goal!

	GOALS	BEHINDS	TOTAL
Westpark Scorpions	6	0	36
Riverside Devils	3	1	19

Only minutes to go in this game, so it looks all over for the Devils. Their crowd has been beaten into silence again. They can't believe it. We can't believe it. And to rub salt into the wound, it was all straight shooting. Six goals and no behinds.

Umpire goes to bounce the ball but as she does the siren goes for the end of the game.

Victory to the Scorpions. They thought they had it in them, but I bet nobody saw nearly a three-goal win coming from the inexperienced Scorpions Under 14s.

You decided that Emma would choose a drop punt.

Emma shoots for goal. Long, long drop punt. Very high and very long. Looks like it's on target. Oh no! At the last minute it clips the inside of the left-hand goal post and it's only a behind. Drop punt was probably the right choice for Emma but there's a slight wind down there blowing from right to left. Emma gets pats on the back as Devils prepare for kick-out.

	GOALS	BEHINDS	TOTAL
Westpark Scorpions	4	1	25
Riverside Devils	2	1	13

Scorps still with a two-goal lead. Good kick-out by the Devils. Out to the back pocket. Then onto a Devils' player, Isla, standing all alone in front of Scorpions' goal. She sells some candy and runs around Thao and out to the wing as easy as you like. Devils players on the loose everywhere. Back into the corridor. Nobody checking Devils. She takes off, takes a bounce, another bounce, finds herself 30 out on her preferred foot and lets a boomer of a kick go and there it is. Sails over the heads of the Scorpions' backs and rolls through. An easy goal for the Devils. Still plenty of time for either team to win this game.

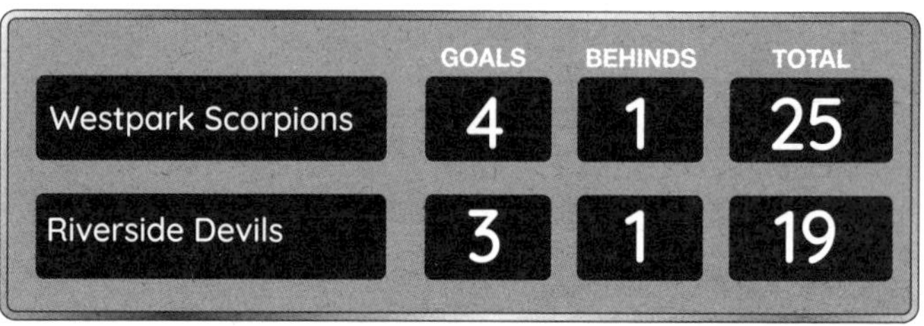

	GOALS	BEHINDS	TOTAL
Westpark Scorpions	4	1	25
Riverside Devils	3	1	19

It'll be interesting to see how the Devils and Scorpions approach the next quarter as the siren goes.

THREE-QUARTER TIME

Scorps gather in the middle of the ground. Coach Rita is not impressed with that last effort, resulting in a Devils' goal. She doesn't put the girls down but is forceful in her instructions. The Scorpions team are quiet as they take in her words. She once again reminds her team of the basics. Focus, pressure, commitment is her message as the girls run to their positions to start the final quarter. It'll be interesting to see what effect her three-quarter time address has on this young side.

FINAL QUARTER

Scorpions are a bit rattled by the quick turnaround by the Devils. They move into position. Looks like the Scorps have decided on a seven-person back line. Probably the right move considering the Devils will have their tails up for this last quarter. Scorps protecting their one-goal lead.

Into the last period of play and Talia has come into the ruck. Heidi down back for safety's sake. Good bounce by the umpire.

Talia goes for a big thump and succeeds in getting the ball into the clear. Sophie with her head over the ball. She'll have to be quick.

Runs backwards and over to Matilda at half-back. She switches play to the other side. Can't hold it up like this. Gives the other side time to set up.

Grace marks and takes off, taking advantage of Devils' lack of speed.

Oh! Now Sophie collects the ball but cops a heavy knock as she kicks and goes down. Thao collects on the run. Kicks. Zoe gets behind the ball, so yes, Zoe takes advantage of the situation, beautiful kick and Elly takes a mark. Nobody on her mark. Doesn't waste time and goes for goal but misses. A behind. Perhaps Elly was a bit too casual there. Mind you, it still could be an important point.

	GOALS	BEHINDS	TOTAL
Westpark Scorpions	4	2	26
Riverside Devils	3	1	19

Meanwhile, back in the middle of the ground, Sophie is still down on the ground. Tries to get up and waves Andy away but she looks pretty concussed.

Yep, Dr Vanessa is out there. Stretcher brought out. Play has stopped.

Devils' gun forward, Belle, has run over to see how Sophie is. They're cousins and Belle is holding Sophie's hand as she's carried off the ground.

A few more of the girls from both sides run up to offer their sympathy. They might be opposing each other here today but none of them like seeing that happen to any player.

Applause from both sides. Unfortunately Sophie won't be returning.

Calm returns but not for long. Ivy has taken Sophie's place ready for the next chapter in this exciting game.

Play resumes. Devils possession to teammate but Ivy cuts across with courage and crashes into her own player. Ball free and Devils get it going. Good interception there by Ava. Now to her sister, Poppy, who swings it wide and now Ruby is free. Takes one bounce. Passes over heads to Grace heading into Scorps forward 50. Short kick to Ruby who's under enormous pressure. Looks like a push in the back to Devils' defender. Pity because everything was working for the Scorpions.

Devils go long. Time running out for a Devils' victory. Devils trap the ball on the boundary. Players working in a phone booth here. Scorpions' half-back, Holly, tracks it along the boundary line, gets hold of it, looks like she's out here, no, but Devils onballer Jo with a huge tackle puts an end to that. Dropping the ball! Free to Devils who goes back and does a monstrous kick into her forward zone. Big pack. Heidi doing her best. Comes to ground. There's Belle. She's a firecracker. Goes bang and that's the goal they needed. She runs behind the goals celebrating, encouraging the crowd in their appreciation. Teammates run from everywhere. And it's a one-point ball game from here with only a minute or so left on the clock.

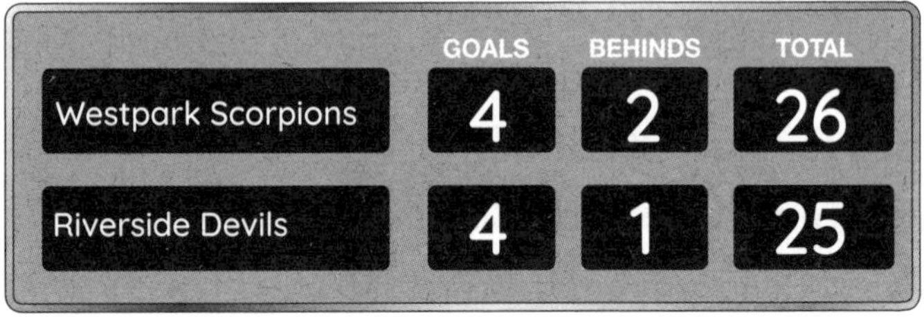

This will test the Scorpions' nerves and concentration, who have basically led all day. Big ruck duel and it gets buried under a pile of very tired bodies. Scorpions getting a number of players behind the ball. Can't get clear ball away. Dribbles. Several players in contention but over the line. Heidi behind in defence.

Ball thrown in. Got to watch out here. That's holding. Free kick to Devils. Short kick but misses its mark. It sits there. Over the line again. Another throw-in and both rucks go at it but neither win the battle.

Ball into space. Scorpions haven't been able to get any run. There's a fumble, a bad fumble. Not much in it. Game's on a knife edge.

Devils pick up the ball with one hand. Long handball over heads. Devils' gun forward Belle has got it. Facing the wrong way to the goals. Kicks over her shoulder. High. High. Goal! It's a goal to the Devils. A come-from-behind victory as the siren ends the game.

Devils elated. Scorpions deflated. Unbelievable.

Coach Rita meets her team as they trudge off the ground. A big lesson learnt today. Some of the team drop their heads. It's a sad way for the Scorpions girls to start the second season. First game back and it's a loss.

FOOTY
DREAMING
Michael Hyde